Clare
the Caring
Fairy

Join the **Rainbow Magic Reading Challenge!**

Read the story and collect your fairy points to climb the
Reading Rainbow at the back of the book.

This book is worth 5 points.

To Zara and Naomi

Special thanks to
Rachel Elliot

ORCHARD BOOKS

First published in Great Britain in 2016 by The Watts Publishing Group

3 5 7 9 10 8 6 4 2

© 2016 Rainbow Magic Limited.
© 2016 HIT Entertainment Limited.
Illustrations © Orchard Books 2016

HIT entertainment

A CIP catalogue record for this book is available from the British Library.

ISBN 978 1 40834 898 7

Printed and bound in Great Britain by Clays Ltd, Elcograf S.p.A.

MIX
Paper from
responsible sources
FSC® C104740
FSC
www.fsc.org

The paper and board used in this book are made from wood from responsible sources

Orchard Books
An imprint of Hachette Children's Group
Part of The Watts Publishing Group Limited
Carmelite House, 50 Victoria Embankment, London EC4Y 0DZ

An Hachette UK Company
www.hachette.co.uk
www.hachettechildrens.co.uk

Clare
the Caring Fairy

by Daisy Meadows

ORCHARD

www.rainbowmagic.co.uk

Jack Frost's Spell

The Friendship Fairies like big smiles.
They want to spread good cheer for miles.
Those pests want people to connect,
And treat each other with respect.

I don't agree! I just don't care!
I want them all to feel despair.
And when their charms belong to me,
Each friend will be an enemy!

Contents

The Last Day

It was a beautiful summer's afternoon on Rainspell Island. Rachel Walker pulled shut the door of the Sunny Days Bed and Breakfast and skipped down the steps. Her best friend Kirsty Tate was waiting for her on the path, and their parents had already started walking towards the park.

"I'm really looking forward to this barbecue," said Rachel. "I'm starving!"

"I think the hot weather makes us hungrier than usual," said Kirsty with a grin. "Just *thinking* about burgers is making my stomach rumble!"

Rachel laughed and reached out to hold Kirsty's hand.

"This has been one of the best holidays ever," she said, as they hurried to catch up with their parents. "I can't believe that we're going home tomorrow."

"Holidays on Rainspell always go too fast," said Kirsty.

The two girls shared a secret smile. Rainspell Island was the place where they had met and become best friends, and where they had had their first adventures with the fairies.

"It's a great idea to celebrate the last day of the Summer Friends Club with a barbecue," said Mr Walker, with a twinkle in his eye. "I love barbecues!"

At the start of their holiday, the girls had joined the Summer Friends Club, a holiday play scheme for children who were staying on the island. Now they had reached the end of their stay, it was time to say goodbye to all their new friends.

"Although it has been a bit harder to make friends than I thought it would be," Kirsty said to Rachel.

11

"I agree," Rachel replied. "It's all because of mean Jack Frost and his goblins. They've caused a lot of mischief."

Walking a little way behind their parents, the girls talked quietly about the adventures they had been sharing with the Friendship Fairies over the last few days.

"It's been non-stop magic since the day we arrived," Kirsty remembered. "Esther the Kindness Fairy whisked us off to Fairyland for a tea party with her and the other Friendship Fairies."

"It would have been lovely if Jack Frost hadn't turned up," Rachel added.

Jack Frost and his goblins had sneakily stolen the fairies' magical objects while no one was looking. He wanted to use them to get lots of friends that he could boss around. And, as long as he had the magical objects, friendships in the human and fairy worlds would suffer.

"Jack Frost loves trying to spoil everyone's fun," said Kirsty. "This time he's really made it difficult for friends to get along. Even Jen and Ginny have fallen out a few times."

Jen and Ginny were the teenage best friends who ran the Summer Friends Club.

"Thank goodness that Florence the Friendship Fairy cast a 'Friends Through Thick and Thin' spell on our friendship bracelets," said Rachel. "I can't imagine ever falling out with you. It would be horrible!"

Kirsty smiled, but she still looked anxious. Ahead, her parents were laughing with Rachel's parents. Even their friendships would be spoiled if Jack Frost could not be stopped.

"Florence said that even the magical bracelets won't hold out for long if the fairies don't get their objects back quickly," she said worriedly. "And there is still one missing – Clare the Caring

Fairy's magical mood ring."

"We have a whole day left to find it," said Rachel. "We've already found the other three – I'm sure we can do it if we try our best."

"We must," said Kirsty. "Without it, the Summer Friends Club barbecue will be a disaster, and friendships everywhere will be ruined!"

Barbecue Bickering

The girls followed their parents into
Rainspell Park, and spotted Heather the
ice-cream seller. She usually sold her ice
cream in the town, but today she had set
up a little stall next to the gravelled path
that ran around the park.

"She must think the park is going to get really busy because of the barbecue," said Rachel with a smile.

They both liked Heather. She was always kind and happy, and she seemed to really love her work.

"Selling ice cream must be one of the best jobs in the world," said Kirsty, as they waved to Heather. "Just imagine being able to eat as much ice cream as you like!"

"I think you'd soon get sick of it," said Mrs Walker, overhearing their conversation.

The girls looked at each other and laughed.

"Never!" they said at the same time.

The barbecue had been set up beside the tepee tent where the club was based. There was already a big crowd of people there, and the delicious aroma of barbecue food wafted over towards them.

"There's Lara!" said Kirsty, spotting one of their new friends from the club.

"Hello, Lara!" called Rachel, walking towards her.

Lara waved at them. She was carrying an ice-cream cone from Heather's stall. As Rachel and Kirsty reached her, Oscar, another friend from the club, pushed into Lara. Her ice cream was knocked out of the cone and fell to the ground.

"Oh, no, look what you've done!" Lara cried out.

"You've ruined my ice cream! I only had one lick of it. You should look where you're going, clumsy!"

"I don't care," said Oscar, with a shrug. "You should have been looking where you were going."

Lara stormed off, and Rachel and Kirsty exchanged a knowing look. Oscar and Lara were not usually bad tempered, but today they didn't seem to care about anyone.

"I know exactly why they are being so mean," said Rachel in a low voice.

21

"Because Jack Frost still has the mood ring, people have stopped caring about each other's feelings."

They walked closer to the barbecue and saw a lovely seating area made from long, thick logs. Several of the other children from the Summer Friends Club were there, but they didn't look very happy. They all had their arms folded, and they were arguing in loud, cross voices about who should sit where. Suddenly there was a crash and a splash. Eric had kicked his football into some drinks and knocked them all to the ground.

"The drinks!" exclaimed an elderly lady. "You should be more careful, young man!"

Eric just smirked at her.

"Why should I?" he asked. "It's not my problem."

He kicked the ball again, and it crashed into the log seats and sent some of them tumbling down.

"What a rude little boy," said the elderly lady.

The girls felt very embarrassed. They knew that Eric wasn't usually rude at all.

"Things are getting worse," Kirsty whispered. "If we don't find the mood ring soon, perhaps Florence's magic will start to wear off and we will start not caring as much about each other's feelings."

The best friends looked at each other in dismay, and then hooked their little fingers together.

"We won't let that happen," said Rachel in a fierce voice. "We will find a way to stop Jack Frost!"

They went to find their parents, who were standing in the busy queue

for the barbecue. All the adults looked
irritated, and a few of them were pushing
the others to try to jump ahead in the
queue. As the girls watched, a couple of
men were nudged aside and Mr Walker
pushed his way out from the crowd. He
had a burger clutched in his hand.

"I got one!" he shouted. "It's the very
last one, and it's all mine!"

Kirsty, Rachel and the other parents all stared at him in astonishment.

"What about burgers for the rest of us?" asked Mrs Walker in a surprised voice.

Mr Walker just shrugged as if he didn't care, and took a big bite of the burger.

"Dad?" asked Rachel in a whisper. "This isn't like you!"

But her dad took no notice. He was usually kind and thoughtful, but right then he seemed like a completely different person. Rachel turned to Kirsty, tears brimming in her eyes.

"What are we going to do?" she cried.

Mystery VIP

Kirsty gave Rachel a hug.

"Come on," she said. "This is all because of Jack Frost, and we *will* find the last magical object and stop him. Let's go and say hello to Jen and Ginny, and then try to decide what to do."

But when they walked up to Jen and Ginny, the teenagers were in the middle of a big argument.

"I don't want to give the silly speech,"
Jen was saying. "I can't be bothered.
What's the point of it, anyway?"

"What speech?" asked Rachel.

Jen and Ginny glanced at her, but they
didn't even smile.

"We've written this speech about the
Summer Friends Club," said Ginny. "All
about how successful it's been and how
much fun we've all had. Blah blah blah."

"*You* can give the speech," Jen went on, glaring at Ginny.

"I don't care about the club or the speech," Ginny snapped back. "You should do it."

They each folded their arms and turned their backs on each other.

Rachel and Kirsty exchanged a worried look.

"Everyone is acting as if they don't care about anyone else," said Rachel, feeling a lump in her throat as she thought about her dad.

31

"Or any*thing*," said Kirsty. "And it's all because of Jack Frost and his goblins."

Jen and Ginny marched off in opposite directions, and Rachel sank down on a nearby log.

"Oh, dear," she said in a gloomy voice. "I'm starting to worry that Jack Frost might really beat us this time."

Suddenly, something beside the log caught her eye. It was a small water cooler, and it was glowing. Rachel jumped to her feet.

"Kirsty!" she cried. "That's magic!"

The girls kneeled down beside the little
water cooler and opened the lid together.
Out fluttered Clare the Caring Fairy,
shivering a little.

"Hello!" she said in a bright voice,
rubbing her hands together. "Thanks for
letting me out – it's so
chilly in there!"

She was
wearing a
playsuit covered
in red roses,
a sky-blue
jacket and a
pair of brown
ankle boots. Her
gleaming auburn
hair hung loosely
to her shoulders.

"Hello, Clare," said Kirsty, feeling excited to see the last of the Friendship Fairies. "You'll soon warm up – it's another hot day here on Rainspell."

Rachel let out a sigh and Clare looked around at the cross faces of the people at the barbecue. A frown creased her forehead.

"It might be a warm day, but the mood

here looks as cold as ice," she said.

"Everyone is grumpy with each other," said Rachel. "They just want everything their own way."

"I have to get my magical mood ring back from Jack Frost and the goblins," said Clare. "It's the only way to make sure that people care about each other again. Please, girls, will you help me?"

"Of course!" said Kirsty and Rachel together.

"Where shall we start looking?" asked Kirsty, glancing around and seeing that the crowd of people had started waving and pointing at someone. "Oh, someone very special must have arrived!"

Rachel looked over too, and saw that Jen and Ginny were fetching a table and chair.

"He's got to be able to sit and eat in comfort," she heard Ginny say to Jen.

A man scurried over to the crowd with an umbrella.

"Are you feeling too hot?" he called out, shoving people aside. "This will shade you from the sun!"

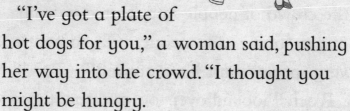

"I've got a plate of hot dogs for you," a woman said, pushing her way into the crowd. "I thought you might be hungry.

"Who *is* this amazing visitor?" asked Kirsty in astonishment.

"Cushions!" voices were calling out. "How is he feeling? Here's a footstool! Let *me* care for him!"

"Can we do anything to make you feel happier?" the girls heard Ginny asking.

"Why does everyone care about this visitor so much?" asked Rachel. "He must be someone very special, to make all these people fuss over him and his feelings."

"Yes," said Kirsty, frowning. "It's even stranger when you think how uncaring they've all been to each other. Who could he be?"

But the crowd was tightly packed around the mystery visitor, and the girls couldn't see anything.

"We have to find out who he is," said Rachel. "But *how*?"

Tempting Jack Frost

"Clare, can you turn us into fairies?"
Kirsty asked in an urgent voice. "If we
fly overhead we should be able to see the
visitor and find out what's going on."

Clare fluttered up and gently rested
her wand against Rachel's golden hair.

Magical sparkles twinkled among the
curls as fairy dust sprinkled down over
her shoulders. She shrank to fairy size as
Clare fluttered over to Kirsty's shoulder
and cast the same spell on her. The girls
smiled at each other as they spread their
wings and flew up into the sky beside
Clare. It was
always exciting
to become a
fairy – even if it
wasn't for a happy
reason.

"Keep out of sight in
the tree branches," said Clare.

From among the leafy branches,
the three fairies gazed down at the
crowd. They were gathered around the
mysterious visitor, and Kirsty gave a gasp

of shock. He had a long beard and long
nose, and he was dressed in a glittery ice
blue polo shirt and shorts. There were
even glittery blue sandals on his big
blue feet.

"It's Jack Frost!" Rachel cried out. "Why is he here in the human world? I thought he'd be in his Ice Castle, trying to keep the magical mood ring away from Clare."

"It looks as if he's trying to make new friends that he can boss around," said Kirsty. "And I think he's succeeding."

All around him, grown-ups and children were fetching and carrying, bowing and doing everything he said.

"Let's get closer," said Clare. "Maybe we can somehow stop him from bossing everyone around."

Staying high above everyone, they fluttered nearer. Clare let out a squeak of surprise and pointed at Jack's hand. A beautiful ring was glimmering on his finger – a ring that seemed to change

colour every time it
moved.

"My
magical mood
ring!" Clare
exclaimed.
"We've found it –
but how are we going
to get it back?

There were too many people around
Jack Frost – someone would be sure
to spot them. Rachel glanced around
and spotted a straggly queue next to
Heather's ice-cream stall.

"I've got an idea," she said. "If we can
get Jack Frost thinking about ice cream,
perhaps he will send some of these people
to fetch one, and we'll have a chance to
get the ring."

The fairies perched on a branch as close to Jack as they could get. There were too many people nearby to be able to get right behind him, but they were near enough for him to hear them if they spoke loudly enough.

"Heather makes the most delicious ice cream I've ever tasted," said Rachel.

"Mmm, it's wonderful," said Kirsty. "The perfect thing for such a hot day."

"The strawberry flavour tastes as juicy as real strawberries," Clare added. "It's so refreshing."

They were watching Jack Frost as they talked, and they saw him lick his lips.

"What else can we do to make you comfortable?" called a voice from the crowd.

"Ice cream," said Jack Frost at once. "A yummy ice cream – strawberry flavour. Now!"

The crowd around him turned and raced off across the park towards Heather's stall. Jack Frost let out a happy sigh and leaned back against the cushions, his hands clasped across his tummy. The sun beat down on his face and his eyes flickered and then closed. A tiny snore escaped his lips.

"This is our chance," Kirsty whispered.
"Let's swoop down and try to slip the
ring off his finger."

"What if he wakes up?" asked Clare,
biting her lip.

"We have to risk it," said Rachel,
squeezing Clare's hand. "Don't be scared
– we'll all be together!"

The fairies flew down and hovered beside Jack Frost's hands. The finger wearing the mood ring was on top.

"All we have to do is slide it off without waking him," Kirsty whispered. "Come on, we can do it!"

They each got a grip on the ring and started to pull as slowly as they could. Luckily, the ring was a little loose on his bony finger. It was possible to move it along without brushing against his skin. They just had to be very careful, and very slow.

But suddenly, there was a rumbling
sound in Jack Frost's chest. Then he let
out a loud burp and opened his eyes.

"Fairies!" he exclaimed. "Get away
from me!"

He swatted at them with his hands.
Clare darted backwards, but Rachel and
Kirsty folded their arms, and hovered just
out of his reach.

"You are causing big problems for everyone," Rachel said. "Give Clare her ring and let everything go back to normal."

"Shan't!" Jack Frost snapped.

He jumped up and ran away from them.

"Quickly, follow him!" Kirsty cried. "We can't let that ring out of our sight!"

True Friendship

Kirsty, Rachel and Clare zoomed after Jack Frost, flying high above him as he sprinted across the park. They watched him run around the park fountain, past the friendship sign on the wall of the tennis clubhouse and right into the tepee where the Summer Friends Club was based.

"Follow him into the tent!" called
Kirsty in an urgent voice. "If we can
corner him in there, perhaps we can find
a way to get the ring back!"

They flew towards the tent opening, but
at the last second Jack Frost slapped the
tent flap shut and tied
it from the inside.
The three fairies
bounced off
and landed
on the
grass with
a bump.
Rachel
glanced
around quickly,
but no one had
spotted them.

"Luckily everyone's either at the barbecue or the ice-cream stall," she said, flying back up to the tent flap and patting on it hard. "Let us in! You can't stay in there for ever!"

"Go away and pester someone else," Jack Frost called.

"I like being the boss of all these new friends, and I'm not giving the ring back, no matter what you say!"

The three fairies stared at each other, and then Rachel clicked her fingers.

"I've got it!" she said. "Jack Frost loves ice cream, and I bet he'd come out of the tent if we could offer him something really amazing."

"No sooner said than done," said Clare, waving her wand.

A large cone of ice cream suddenly appeared on the grass outside the tent, standing in its own special holder. The cone was glittering blue and the ice cream was as white as frost, with sparkling blue sauce cascading over the top.

"That is a beautiful cone of ice cream," said Kirsty in a loud voice.

"It's so blue and glittery. I bet it tastes amazing."

"It's blueberry cream flavour," said Clare. "It's bursting with the taste of real, juicy blueberries and rich, smooth vanilla. The cone is made of sugar and popping candy."

The fairies saw the tent flap open slightly. One suspicious eye peered out at the ice cream.

"Get ready," Rachel whispered. Suddenly, Jack Frost's hand shot out through the tent flap.

As he grabbed the ice cream, Kirsty and Clare threw their arms around his wrist, holding on as tightly as they could while Rachel tugged on the ring.

Jack Frost twisted his arm and roared with fury, but Rachel was strong and determined. Just as Jack Frost finally wrenched his hand away from the fairies, the ring came off in Rachel's hands. She handed it to Clare and it shrank to fairy size instantly.

"You tricky, sneaky fairies!" Jack Frost screeched, charging out of the tent like an angry bull.

"We were only taking back what belongs to Clare," said Kirsty, joining hands with Rachel and Clare. "You obviously don't know very much about true friends."

"Oh, yes, I do," said Jack Frost in an offended voice. "I've just made lots of new friends. They all want to look after me. They just went to get me some ice cream."

He looked down at the ice cream in his hand and gave it a big lick.

"But friendship isn't about giving orders," said Rachel. "You can't just boss your friends around and expect to get your own way all the time."

Jack Frost's mouth fell open in surprise. "Why not?" he demanded.

"Because *everyone's* feelings are important," said Clare. "Not just yours. True friends care about each other and are kind to each other. That's what real friendship is."

"Real friendship is about always having someone standing beside you, ready to help," Kirsty added.

Jack Frost took another lick of his ice

cream. He looked very thoughtful.

"I like the sound of that," he said in a quiet voice. "I wish I had some real friends."

He gobbled down the rest of his ice cream. Rachel, Kirsty and Clare exchanged surprised glances.

"This doesn't sound like Jack Frost!" said Rachel.

"It's a pity my plan didn't work," Jack Frost went on. "I liked having humans waiting on me hand and foot. But now I know the secret, I'm going to be the best friend of all time!"

"What do you mean?" Clare asked.

Something strange was happening to Jack Frost's face. It was something that Rachel and Kirsty had hardly ever seen before.

"He's *smiling*," Kirsty whispered, hardly able to believe her eyes. "He's really smiling a proper smile – a caring smile!"

"I'm going to throw a party," said Jack Frost, rubbing his hands together. "I'm going to invite all my goblin friends. And they love ice cream just as much as I do, so it'll be an ice-cream party!"

The three fairies didn't know what to say. They just gazed at him in amazement. They had never heard him being so friendly.

"Do you like ice cream, too?" he asked.

They nodded, and Jack Frost opened his arms wide.

"Then you are all invited – together with the other Friendship Fairies, of course. Let's have a party to celebrate real friendship!"

Clare still seemed to be too surprised to move, but Rachel and Kirsty fluttered forward, smiling.

"We'd love to come," they said.

Jack Frost grinned and disappeared with a flash of blue lightning.

Laughing in surprise and delight, Clare lifted her wand. Rachel and Kirsty saw her mood ring glittering on her finger.

"Come on, we have to go to Fairyland and find the other Friendship Fairies," Clare said. "We've got a party to attend!"

A Surprising Party

The party at the Ice Castle was in full swing by the time Rachel and Kirsty arrived with the Friendship Fairies. The castle door was wide open, and glittering blue lights adorned every turret. Arm in arm, the girls fluttered in with Esther, Mary, Mimi and Clare. Florence the Friendship Fairy and Becky the Best Friend Fairy were close behind them.

The Gobolicious Band was playing a lively tune, and there were tables set up all around the courtyard for guests to make their own ice-cream sundaes. Huge bowls were dotted around the tables, filled with every colour of ice cream that Rachel and Kirsty could imagine. Some goblins were dancing, some were squawking at each other, but most were making tall sundaes and gobbling them down as fast as they could.

Jack Frost spotted the fairies and came hurrying through the crowd of guests.

"Welcome to my party!" he said, with a beaming smile. "What sort of ice cream would you like?"

He scooped up ice cream for them all and led them towards the tables.

"Come over here," he said. "Make

sundaes and then eat them and then dance, all right?"

Rachel and Kirsty couldn't help but smile as he turned to greet the next guests. Even though he sounded bossy, they knew that Jack Frost was trying his best to be a good host.

"How are you?" they heard him demanding of a small, pimply goblin.

"Tell me your favourite ice cream. Quick!"

"It's amazing," said Rachel. "Jack Frost is really trying hard to be a caring friend."

"I guess Clare's mood ring worked its magic on him without him knowing it," said Kirsty.

Side by side, they created glorious ice-cream sundaes in a rainbow of colours, topped with sprinkles of nuts.

"We can't thank you enough for all your help," said Clare, as they all dipped into their ice creams with long spoons.

"We could never have imagined that our adventures would end with a party here in the Ice Castle!" Mimi added. "It's all thanks to you."

"We care about all our fairy friends,"

said Kirsty. "We just want you to be happy."

Esther and Mary stepped forward and gave each of the girls a tiny silver charm. Each was shaped like a fairy in mid-flight.

"They are to add to your friendship bracelets," Esther explained.

"They're to show that you are best friends to all the fairies," Mary added.

Thrilled, the girls fitted the charms to their bracelets and hugged the fairies.

"We've had lots of fun," said Rachel. "I hope we'll see you again soon."

"True friends are always together in their hearts," said Florence.

Smiling, Becky raised her wand and the world seemed to shimmer around them. Sparkling fairy dust lifted Rachel and Kirsty into the air. They blinked, and found that they were standing in Rainspell Park, close to the barbecue party. The sound of laughter and happy conversation filled the air.

"There you are, girls," called Mr Walker. "I'm just going to get some more burgers so that everyone can have one."

"OK, Dad," said Rachel, giving him a big smile.

Everything was back to normal. Oscar and Lara came running towards them, hand in hand.

"Look what we've made together," said Lara.

Oscar held out two badges with 'Summer Friends Club' printed on them.

"They're special badges for everyone in the club," said Oscar. "And we were hoping that you both might agree to be pen pals with us, so we can stay friends after we leave the island."

"We don't want to lose touch with the wonderful new friends we've made," Lara added.

"We'd love to," said Rachel and Kirsty together.

Suddenly, a microphone squealed, and Jen stepped up onto a hay bale with Ginny at her side.

"We're absolutely delighted to see so many of our friends here today," said Jen, gazing around at the crowd. "Thank you for coming."

"We've really enjoyed running the Summer Friends Club together," Ginny went on. "We've made lots of new friends and had heaps of fun along the way. We thought that we would be teaching you, but actually *you* have taught *us* the meaning of friendship."

"We care about each and every one of you," Jen continued. "We will never forget our amazing summer, and we hope that you will be back on Rainspell again next year."

"We can't wait!" Ginny finished.

There was a roar of applause, and the teenage best friends stepped down from the hay bale. Rachel and Kirsty ran over to them.

"That was a lovely, caring speech," said Rachel.

Jen and Ginny hugged them.

"You two are amazing," said Jen. "You're such a fantastic example of a true friendship. I've never seen you get cross with each other."

"And you always listen to each other's point of view," Ginny added. "We're going to try to be more like you in future."

Rachel and Kirsty felt a bit embarrassed, but very pleased. They shared a secret, happy smile and linked their little fingers together.

"I'm so happy that I met you here on Rainspell," Kirsty said. "Isn't it wonderful that we've been best friends ever since?"

"And that won't ever change," said Rachel, smiling. "Best friends for ever!"

The End

Now it's time for Kirsty and Rachel to help...

Fizz the Fireworks Fairy

Read on for a sneak peek...

"I am SO excited!" Rachel Walker said to her best friend, Kirsty Tate.

"Me, too!" Kirsty replied with a grin. Then she whispered quietly, "I wonder if we'll have any fairy adventures."

The girls were on their way to visit Kirsty's grandparents for Fireworks Night. The two best friends always had fun on their trips together, but they also had a special secret – they were friends with the fairies! They had shared many magical adventures together since they had first met on Rainspell Island.

"You girls are going to have a great

time," said Mrs Tate, from the passenger seat. "My parents are so looking forward to having you. And Sundown Village Fireworks Festival is the best in the world! There'll be a cupcake party, a parade and then a huge fireworks display on the night itself."

"I can't wait!" Rachel exclaimed.

Mr Tate looked at them in the rear-view mirror. "I wish we could stay the whole week, but your grandparents will take good care of you."

"You'll be back for the fireworks, won't you?" Kirsty asked.

"We wouldn't miss it," Mr Tate promised.

The next thing they knew, everyone was piling out of the Tates' car and heading to the door of a beautiful cottage. There was a pathway with large stepping stones, and an ivy-covered arch over the doorway. The roof was even covered in grass!

As Rachel closed her car door, she heard a strange noise – like a tiny, tiny firework.

"Did you hear that?" she asked Kirsty, looking around.

Kirsty shook her head.

Read Fizz the Fireworks Fairy to find out what adventures are in store for Kirsty and Rachel!

Competition!

The Friendship Fairies have created a special
competition just for you!

Collect all four books in the Friendship Fairies series
and answer the special questions in the back of each one.

Rachel and Kirsty have lots of
fun at the _ _ _ _ _ _
Friends Club

Once you have all four answers, take the first letter from
each one and arrange them to spell a secret word!
When you have the answer, go online and enter!

We will put all the correct entries into a draw and select
a winner to receive a special Rainbow Magic Goody Bag
featuring lots of treats for you and your fairy friends.
The winner will also feature in a new Rainbow Magic story!

Enter online now at www.rainbowmagicbooks.co.uk

Calling all parents, carers and teachers!
The Rainbow Magic fairies are here to help
your child enter the magical world of reading.
Whatever reading stage they are at, there's
a Rainbow Magic book for everyone!
Here is Lydia the Reading Fairy's guide to
supporting your child's journey at all levels.

Starting Out

1 Our Rainbow Magic Beginner Readers are perfect for first-time readers who are just beginning to develop reading skills and confidence. Approved by teachers, they contain a full range of educational levelling, as well as lively full-colour illustrations.

Developing Readers

2 Rainbow Magic Early Readers contain longer stories and wider vocabulary for building stamina and growing confidence. These are adaptations of our most popular Rainbow Magic stories, specially developed for younger readers in conjunction with an Early Years reading consultant, with full-colour illustrations.

Going Solo

3 The Rainbow Magic chapter books - a mixture of series and one-off specials - contain accessible writing to encourage your child to venture into reading independently. These highly collectible and much-loved magical stories inspire a love of reading to last a lifetime.

www.rainbowmagicbooks.co.uk

"Rainbow Magic got my daughter reading chapter books. Great sparkly covers, cute fairies and traditional stories full of magic that she found impossible to put down" - Mother of Edie (6 years)

"Florence LOVES the Rainbow Magic books. She really enjoys reading now" Mother of Florence (6 years)

The Rainbow Magic Reading Challenge

Well done, fairy friend – you have completed the book!
This book was worth 5 points.

See how far you have climbed on the **Reading Rainbow**
on the Rainbow Magic website below.

The more books you read, the more points you will get,
and the closer you will be to becoming a Fairy Princess!

How to get your Reading Rainbow
1. Cut out the coin below
2. Go to the Rainbow Magic website
3. Download and print out your poster
4. Add your coin and climb up the Reading Rainbow!

There's all this and lots more at
www.rainbowmagicbooks.co.uk

You'll find activities, competitions, stories, a special
newsletter and complete profiles of all the
Rainbow Magic fairies. Find a fairy with your name!